Slide!

Slide by Ron Stout

Copyright © 2023 Ron Stout.

ISBN-13: 979-8-9862935-2-3

Published by Ron Stout Books
Wilcox, AZ

Editing by ChristianEditingAndDesign.com

Front Cover and Interior Artwork by Kim Merritt

This is a work of fiction. Any resemblance of fictional characters to persons living or dead is strictly coincidental.

Slide!

by RON STOUT

Contents

Chapter 1

The Blowout: The Eagles

Sheridan Matthews stood in the third-base coaching box looking calm and collected but churning and seething inside. *Just what else,* she wondered, *can go wrong? Nothing has been right since the first pitch of this game.*

Sheridan was the first-year coach of the Mountain Shadows High School Mountaineers, and they were playing her old alma mater, Eagle Rock, for the first time since she took over the reins. She did *so* want to win this one! But a glance at the scoreboard showed the Eagles had scored in every inning and were leading now in the top of fifth by 13-1. Ouch! They were in real danger of the "mercy rule" —calling the game over because the scores are more than ten runs apart.

Coming up this inning was the middle to bottom of her lineup (5, 6, 7: Abby, Sandy, and Leenie).

It would be nice if they could get something going, she mused. *After all, we only have three more outs and this one is over. That little girl pitching for Eagle Rock puts something incredible on the ball. It actually looks as though it is rising when it comes down. She is a treasure and will probably get a bid from a top college. She will get my vote for All-League."*

Abby, actually Abigail Anderson, was a big, strong third baseman, one of the two black power hitters on the team. She stepped into the batter's box. The Eagle Rock pitcher, a girl named Shirley Webb, went into her wind-up . . . and *whoosh!*

"Steeee-rike!" the umpire bellowed as Abby stood stoically with the bat on her shoulder. After the pitch, she stepped out.

Webb watched the catcher, waiting for Abby to step back into the batter's box. Abby looked down at Sheridan, and for the third time, Sheridan gave her the "hit away" sign.

Webb wound up and delivered. Abby took a gigantic cut at it — a swing and a miss. Strike two.

Again, Webb wound up and delivered. Abby swung and connected, but the ball went straight up in the air — seemed like half a mile, but an easy out. One down.

Sandra Sanderson — could she be called anything except "Sandy"? — came to the plate. She had been standing in the on-deck circle swinging three bats. Her big hands could handle them. She checked with Sheridan, picked up the sign to hit away, and moved into the batter's box.

Webb delivered. "Ball," cried the umpire.

The next pitch came in. "Steeee-rike!" Sandy watched it whiff by.

Shirley set up again and delivered. Sandy stepped into the pitch and hit it hard but smacked it right to the shortstop on the fly. Two down.

RON STOUT

Darlene Travis stepped out of the on-deck circle and walked to the plate. The youngest of the girls, just a freshman, she had little experience. Her two biggest assets: she could run extremely fast and she took training seriously. She was popular with the girls, who called her "Leenie."

Leenie stepped in and swung at the first pitch, sending it foul down the first-base line. The next pitch was outside. Then came a fastball down the chute, and Leenie swung hard again, missing the pitch. Down to one last strike, Leenie stepped out, swung her bat nervously back and forth, adjusted her grip, and looked down at the coach, who was standing still, looking at her. She stepped in.

Webb wound up and *whoosh.* "Steeee-rike three!" yelled the umpire. Leenie watched, her bat on her shoulder. She took a third strike. *Oh, no,* Sheridan thought. *Won't they ever learn? You don't take third strikes! Whether the game is on the line or we are behind thirteen runs, you don't take a third strike. Rats!*

Game over. The girls from both teams came out of the dugouts, lined up from opposite sides, and walked toward each other exchanging high fives. The Eagle Rock players were smiling—the Mountain Shadows players were not.

The team gathered around Sheridan, and she spoke with an enthusiasm she did not feel. "Okay, gang. Let's shake this one off and get back to work. Tomorrow, practice as usual at three-thirty—don't be late."

Back in the coaches' office, Sheridan sat and pondered what she needed to do to get this team rolling. The talent was there, but there was no spark, no life, no fire. She needed a leader. What to do?

9

Slide!

Sheridan looked over her roster sheet for the jillionth time. It just didn't seem as if any of them would emerge as an on-fire leader. She stared off into the distance and tried to visualize just how these girls might come together as a team. Nothing materialized.

She glanced down again at the card with the batting order she had more or less settled on.

Batting Order

1. 2 - Lopez, Maria, Giant - Jr. - 2nd - L/R
2. 7 - Watkins, Crystal, Crissy - So. - LF - S/R
3. 5 - Thomason, Sally, Tiny - Sr. - 1st - L/L
4. 00 - Norton, Shawnaray, Beast - Sr. - CF - S/R
5. 6 - Anderson, Abigail, Abby - Sr. - 3rd - R/R
6. 22 - Sanderson, Sandra, Sandy - Jr. - SS - R/R
7. 11 - Travis, Darlene , Leenie - F - RF - R/R
8. 14 - Cornwell, Elizabeth, Liz - Sr. - C - R/R
9. 1 - Mason, Mickey, Mickey - Sr. - P - L/L

Other Players

12 - Farnesi, Sharon - So. - U - R/R

17 - Whitley, Alison - So. - OF - R/R

19 - Smalley, Patricia - Jr. - U - S/R

25 - Winters, Rebecca - Sr. - OF - R/R

Nothing. She came up with nothing.

CHAPTER 2

Melody: The New Girl

Melody Gray stepped into the coach's office, clutching her transfer and enrollment papers. Approaching one of the assistants perched behind a desk, she said, "Hello, I am here to see Coach Matthews, please."

"Looks as though you are transferring in," the assistant commented.

"Yes, ma'am."

"Coach Matthews just went down to the admin building. Do you want to wait? She said she would be back in a few moments."

"Sure. Guess I will," Melody responded.

"Go ahead and take a seat."

The door swung open and Sheridan breezed in, noting the girl quietly waiting. Turning to her before the assistant could say anything, the coach asked, "Are you waiting to see me? I'm Coach Matthews, the softball coach."

"My name is Melody Gray, Coach, and I am transferring in from Indiana. I would like to try out for your softball team."

"Wonderful! Come on in and sit down."

As they settled in Sheridan's office, she continued. "Let me ask you a few questions. How long have you been playing ball?"

"Since I was nine years old. I played in the tweenie leagues, then ASA ball. Last season I played on the freshman team at Lincoln High School in my little Indiana town."

Sheridan went on. "Right or left hander?"

"Switch batter — throw right"

"How tall are you?"

"Five feet, ten inches — one hundred sixty pounds dripping wet."

"Good. What position are you most comfortable at?" Sheridan asked.

Melody, grinning broadly, said, "Yes."

Sheridan raised her eyebrows and looked up, saw the grin, and responded with one of her own.

"Paper here says you are a sophomore. If we put number fifteen on your back, is that okay?"

"Yes, ma'am."

Sheridan was scribbling on her notepad: 15 - Gray, Melody - So. - Util - S/R

"Oh, do you have your shoes and mitt?"

"Yes, ma'am."

12

"Do you have your own bat?"

"Sure do—an aluminum one."

"Okay. Come on down to the gym about three o'clock. We will issue you practice uniforms and . . ."

At 3:00 sharp, Melody hurried into the gym. Spotting her, the coach took her over to the manager for a locker, uniforms, towels, and whatever she needed.

When Melody walked out onto the field, Abby turned to Shawnaray Norton, whom everyone called the Beast, and asked, "Who is that big white girl?"

"I dunno," Beast answered.

"Looks like she is going to join us," Abby remarked.

"Hey, everyone," Coach Matthews said in a raised voice. "This here's Melody Gray. She's transferring in and will be trying out for the team. Give her a good old western welcome."

The infield took their positions. The assistant coach started popping little grounders down to them that they picked up and fired to first. Sheridan took the outfielders, including Melody, out to the grass and started sending pop flies out to one of them at a time. When Melody's turn came, Sheridan really popped it. Melody set off on the run, ran it down, and caught it. After the catch, she took a couple of hop steps and fired the ball back in sharply. Everyone took notice. Impressive.

While standing in line waiting for their next pop fly, Crissy Watkins sidled up to Melody. "Nice catch, honey. It looked good. I particularly liked your throw back."

"Thank you."

"Where are you from?" Crissy asked.

"A small town in Indiana."

"Been playing ball a lot?"

"All my life," Melody answered.

"Me, too." Crissy inquired, "Which direction do you live from here?"

"About six miles north," Melody said.

"Do you have a car?"

"No."

"Would you like a ride after practice? I can take you home in my buggy."

"Okay, sounds good," Melody replied.

———

During the practice, Coach put Melody in center field to see what she had. Fly ball after fly ball was sent out her way, and she didn't disappoint. She chased all of them down and caught them when possible, picked them up when she couldn't possibly get there. She was so incredibly fast that she was behind the other fielders, waiting to back them up, when the ball was hit out their way.

Everyone was impressed. After practice, Coach came into the locker room and asked Melody to stop by her office on her way out. Beast stood there smoldering. She feared she was losing her position to this new girl. That fear triggered a rapid flow of resentment.

After showering and dressing, Melody appeared at the office door. Sheridan smiled and said, "I was impressed today, Melody, and feel you will fit on this team really well. We'll look for you tomorrow."

"Thank you, Coach."

Melody walked out and turned the corner. She stopped abruptly. Several large, mean-looking black girls blocked her way. She turned to go back and found two of them behind her. She was trapped!

"Hey, bitch, we don't wan' no players comin' in her-ah showun our frens up. Yah herah?" the leader warned.

"Yah," said another. "Who you fink you are, little miss goodie two-shoes?"

One of the black girls charged forward and shoved Melody backward over another girl who had ducked down behind her. A third girl jumped on her and started pummeling her with her fists.

Melody was screaming frantically for help. About that time, Liz — the catcher — and Crissy came around the corner. They saw what was happening and waded right in. It became a free-for-all. Screaming and yelling, hitting with fists, pulling hair, biting — really a mess. At the height of the melee, a shrill whistle sounded repeatedly. School security took charge. They arrested three black girls and all three whites.

Melody got her first ride in a paddy wagon.

CHAPTER 3

Leenie: The Freshman

Coach Sheridan set the phone down on her desk. The superintendent had just told her about the brouhaha created by her players out on the street the night before. What a way to start the day! The administration felt the police had handled the situation well and that things would be quiet from then on. Their best advice to her was not to mention the scene in the hope it would go away. After pondering their suggestion, she decided to let it go for the time being. However, down deep inside she realized the matter would have to be dealt with sooner or later.

Darlene was the only girl in her class to make the varsity softball team. All the others were on the JV. She was awed by these older girls and their talents. The coaches chose her primarily because of her size and speed. While everyone seemed to like her, she didn't have much to say. Somewhere along the way, they started calling her "Leenie," and the name stuck.

When Melody appeared, Leenie smiled at her, and Mel gave her a genuine smile in return. Searching for a conversation opener, Leenie asked, "Have you seen our game schedule for the season?"

"No, I haven't. I wouldn't know any of the other teams anyway."

"Of course. I wasn't thinking. What position do you play?"

"Actually, any of them. I just love softball," Mel answered.

"Coach has me in right field," Leenie offered.

"I don't pitch."

"Neither do I."

"I think I have played every other position at one time or another, though, except pitcher."

"Where do you live?" Leenie inquired.

"Up north of here in the Atwater district."

"Oh, I go to church up there. Grace Chapel."

"What denomination is that?"

"Oh, it's non-denominational. Would you like to go with me Sunday?"

Melody thought about it. "Yes, I would like that. I'll get the time and directions from you later."

———————

Coach Sheridan called them together and told them to sit on the grass. She gave the starting lineups for the next day's game with North Medfield.

Catcher: Liz	Second Base: Maria
First Base: Sally	Third Base: Abby
Shortstop: Sandy	Center Field: Shawnaray
Left Field: Crissy	Right Field: Melody

Pitcher: Mickey

She named Melody for right field! Leenie was terribly disappointed, but she took it well. She turned and wished Melody well. Mel thanked her.

Beast smiled to herself. Coach would not call her Beast, but everyone else did. Occasionally the thought crossed her mind that she was called Beast not because she was so aggressive and physical but because she was so ugly. Every time that thought surfaced, Shawnaray descended into a dark mood. This was one of those times. She sat and smoldered. *I'll have to play next to that stuck-up honkie Melody tomorrow.*

"Hey, Superstar," Caroline cheerfully called to her big sister, Beast."We walking home tahgither tonight?"

"Sure, peewee. Are you ready to go?"

"Aren't yew gonna shower?"

"Naw, let's go."

The two of them walked off then with Beast's hand on Caroline's shoulder. These sisters were fast friends. Despite the six and a half years difference in their ages, they had become close. Their mom worked long hours and was seldom there for them. They didn't even know who their dad was—he had left years before when Caroline was just a baby.

Leenie watched them go and wondered about their home life, their activities, and their family. She was a little afraid of Beast, but she really liked Caroline.

19

CHAPTER 4

Central Valley: The Mustangs

The game was away at Central Valley High. It was a Tuesday afternoon, and Mickey appeared sharp. Her fastball was zinging in there, her rise ball had pepper on it, and her curve was dropping away beautifully. She had the CV batters pretty well stymied.

Leading off the second inning, Crissy hit a single into left center. The next batter, Sandy, hit a ground ball to third, who scooped it up and tried for a double play but got only the runner at second. So, one out and Sandy on first. The batter stepping in was the catcher, Liz. She picked up the sign from Sheridan for a hit-and-run.

Sandy was off like a shot from first at the pitcher's release of the ball. Liz then proceeded to blast the first pitch deep to right center. The right fielder took the ball on the first hop and fired a beautiful, accurate throw to third. As Sandy had rounded second and was already bearing down on third, Sheridan gave her the slide sign. Get down—that throw was coming in true.

What happened next, no one was sure—it all happened so fast. Sandy hit the dirt in a slide under a cloud of dust. A sharp, shrill scream penetrated the air. It looked as if Sandy would have beaten the throw, but her leg doubled up under her in an awkward way and she missed the bag. There was no question she was in extreme agony as she lay there writhing. Nobody but the umpire noticed she was tagged out.

While everyone came running, Sheridan was right there talking to Sandy, telling her not to move. Arriving at a run, Melody and Leenie stood close to her. Sally offered to help.

A glimpse of the injured leg sticking out at a crazy angle convinced all of them it was broken. The athletic director of Central Valley had already called 911 for an ambulance. As the ambulance was only five minutes away, they decided to keep her quiet on the ground until it arrived.

The pain set in and Sandy started to cry. She wasn't alone. Tears trickled down the faces of all the team members. Leenie thought she heard the wail of the ambulance coming closer—and the tears flowed more freely.

The attendants were kind. After talking to Sandy for what seemed like hours, they gently straightened out her leg and put it in a field cast to immobilize it. Then they moved her, slowly and carefully, onto a gurney. She was loaded into the vehicle, the lights and siren came on, and off they went.

During this time, Sheridan had been manipulating her lineup. She shifted Melody to shortstop and inserted Leenie into right field. The game resumed.

———————

The score was 3-0, Mountaineers, when Leenie came up in the top of the sixth. She was feverishly excited but kept telling herself to be calm. She calmed herself so much she took a first strike. *Oh, oh. Can't let that happen.* So she swung on the next pitch, which was almost in the dirt. *Oh, my, what will the coach think?* The third and fourth pitches were outside and low, trying to get her to sucker and strike out, but Leenie had learned her lesson.

With the count 2-2, the CV pitcher tried a change-up. For some reason, Leenie was expecting it, and she slammed the ball deep into left field. For a second it looked as if it would go over, but then it fell inside for a stand-up double. It was her first varsity hit and her teammates enthusiastically cheered her. On top of that, Abby singled her home. Coach gave her a high-five as she trotted back to the dugout.

Melody sidled up to Leenie in the dugout and gave her special congratulations on her first varsity hit. Everyone hated the way she got in the game but were happy she had made the most of it.

———————

After winning the game, the girls' ride home on the bus was uneventful. They talked about Sandy and wondered how she was doing and what was happening. The girls noticed Leenie with her head bowed and eyes closed for a long time. Melody thought she may be praying for Sandy. And she was.

Slide!

Wednesday morning at school, the word quickly circulated that Sandy was in the hospital with a broken leg. She would not be released right away because they were going to do surgery on her leg. She might not be able to return to school for a while. All doubt disappeared. She was out for the season—not something Sheridan wanted to hear.

CHAPTER 5

North Medfield: The Gauchos

A couple of weeks had passed since the Central Valley game. Sandy was back in school getting around on crutches. She kept a good attitude and was always in the dugout during the games. They had won at Indian Wells and Northern Forest—both games without incident. Tension and friction still brewed between Beast and Melody. Sometimes Beast would "accidentally" bump into Melody hard or step on her foot—things like that.

The North Medfield Lady Gauchos scored a run off Mickey in the first inning. A single, a walk, and a batter hit by pitch loaded the bases with only one out. The next batter dropped a bunt down the first baseline and the only play was to first. Run scored. Two down. Mickey got out of the inning with a strikeout. Sheridan watched Mickey returning to the dugout. The girl seemed distracted.

The Mountaineers were not able to place anyone on base in their half of the inning. And so it went. Second inning—no hits, no runs, no errors, either team. Third inning – no hits, no runs, no errors, either team. Mickey seemed to be loosening up and hitting her stride. Only two balls were hit out of the infield—one to Crissy in left and the other to Beast in left center. Everything else was either on the infield or strikeouts.

In the fourth inning, a Gaucho batter hit a high, shallow fly to right center. Beast came charging furiously, and Melody was on the move toward it, both closing in fast. Beast was calling for it, so Melody backed off. At the last minute, Beast stopped and backed away, telling Mel, "It's yours." Mel lunged for it, but there was no way she could catch it at that late time, and the ball dropped in for a single. Mel felt that play was deliberate on Beast's part, but Beast feigned innocence.

"It was your ball all the way."

"No, it wasn't. You were calling for it," Mel yelled.

"Not true. You just couldn't make the play," Beast retorted angrily.

Melody just turned and walked away, silently seething. She was beginning to realize this black girl had it in for her, but she wasn't sure why.

———————

At the end of the inning, Coach pulled Mel aside and asked her privately what had happened out there. Mel glanced at Beast sitting down at the end of the bench glaring at her. Mel turned away and told the coach about the entire episode—what had happened and that she thought she had been set up by Beast.

The Mountaineers lost the ball game 2-0 because the Lady Gauchos got another run in the top of the seventh. They had lost few games, but Sheridan was worried she had problems. First, her pitcher seemed to be distracted or distant—definitely not focused. Something just wasn't right. Second, there seemed to be some serious racial tension on the team. She needed to deal with both these issues, but she wanted to take the right approach. She just wasn't sure what the right approach was.

———

They had the following day off, but the team practiced again on Monday. In the intra-squad game, Melody and Beast were on opposite sides. After Beast got on with a single, the next batter hit a slow ground ball to the left of the second baseman. Maria fielded it and tossed it to Melody just as Beast came flying in with her spikes in the air aimed at Melody. She connected, and Mel was hurt. In fact, she had to take a little time walking off the pain.

At the end of the inning, Sheridan shifted the lineups, which landed Beast and Melody on the same team. In the next inning, the batter hit a shallow fly ball to left center. This time Melody started quickly back-pedaling while Beast charged forward toward the ball. Beast hit Melody in the middle of the back at full speed, and they both went down.

That did it!

Melody came up swinging. She was all over Beast. At first Beast was bewildered, but she quickly recovered and started hitting back viciously. They were really going at it—punching, screaming, yelling, and kicking.

27

Slide!

Sheridan's whistle overrode the melee. The fighting girls were pulled away from each other but continued exchanging curses.

"That's enough," Sheridan shouted. "Stop it!"

More whistle finally ended the confrontation.

———————

In the locker room, Sheridan announced there would be a team meeting at 3:30 the next day. Attendance required.

CHAPTER 6

The Meeting: Coach Matthews

The practice field was across from the school on the city playground property. There were four ball diamonds—two hardball and two softball. On the perimeter was a long hedge with wings here and there where groups could assemble in semi-privacy for team meetings, picnics, or whatever. Sheridan chose one of these enclosures for her meeting. She asked the entire team to come in and sit down. As there were no chairs or benches, they sat cross-legged on the grass. Little Caroline slipped in the back and sat down too. As batgirl, she was readily accepted with the team.

"I have called this meeting," Sheridan began, "because I am not happy with what I am seeing on this team." She stopped to let that sink in. Turning and walking over to the side, she continued, "What I see is one of the world's most divisive issues rearing its ugly head here—and we have no room for it.

Slide!

"Some people in this country love to divide others: the rich against the poor, one political party against the other, educated folks against non-educated folks, the 'haves' against the 'have-nots,' and just about every double-faceted area you can think of. But one of the most dangerous, foolish, and destructive divisions is racial. Dividing by color and breeding hate.

"I feel that multiculturalism promotes this kind of division, but our pledge of allegiance says, 'One Nation, under God, **indivisible** . . .'

That means that we don't divide, we don't segregate, we don't separate. Indivisible . . . we are ONE. That means that we have . . .

NO Anglo-Americans,

NO African-Americans,

NO Latin-Americans,

NO Asian-Americans,

NO Native-Americans.

We are all just <u>AMERICANS</u> — do you get it?"

Melody shifted uneasily and glanced up at Beast, who sat stoically looking forward with no expression on her face. Abby gazed at her feet, and Mickey just stared into space with a tired expression on her face.

Sheridan lowered her voice. "America has been called the great melting pot. Melting means amalgamation—two or more substances melted down and put together to form a completely different substance. Do you know what steel is? It is an amalgam. A mixture of different substances. Iron is not very hard, but when it is melted down with other substances, it becomes rock hard and can be cast into weapons—weapons that win wars!"

30

"What is put with this iron to make it so hard?" she continued, pacing back and forth. "Carbon, manganese, chromium, vanadium, and tungsten. These metals melted into the iron make it **STEEL**."

"And what makes the great American melting pot the hardest, toughest fighting machine in the world? The whites, the blacks, the Hispanics, the Orientals, the Indians — *melted together as one people!* We are not divided — we are ONE."

Sally and Maria both fidgeted, and Leenie's eyes glistened with tears. Crissy, eyes closed, wondered where Sheridan was going with this.

Sheridan was rolling now. "There are those multiculturalists who don't want to make steel but want to make salad out of us. Salad, like steel, is a five-letter word. Like steel, it is made up of several different ingredients. But salad ingredients are chopped up and mixed together. They do not melt into a single product but become just a mixture of lettuce, cucumbers, tomatoes, onions, radishes, and what have you. They may be all mixed up, but they will never be one product. Lettuce will always be lettuce in the salad, tomatoes will always be tomatoes. Get it? They don't meld together — they just mix.

"As Americans, we are NOT mixed together — we are melted. We are not salad — we are steel. Get rid of this multicultural idea," Sheridan concluded.

Total silence. Not a word.

The girls had gathered on the grass in groups. Whites with whites. Blacks with blacks. Now everyone's head hung low as they stared at the ground.

As all this was sinking in, a tiny voice in the back broke the silence, sweetly singing.

Jesus luvs da liddle childrin,

31

Slide!

All the childrin of da worl

Red an yella, brack an white

Dey are preshus in His sight

Jesus luvs da liddle childrin of da worl.

Caroline stopped singing and they all sat in silence for a long time. *How appropriate,* Sheridan thought. *Caroline, in her way, has brought the anger and fighting issue back to a "love" foundation. How appropriate.*

Finally, Sheridan picked it up again. "Now, as a team, we have been doing well. We are on the road to State and the finals. I have a strong feeling we are going to make it — but we will *only* make it if we stop bickering, and baiting, and fighting among ourselves. So, I am not asking you here, **I am telling you — STOP IT!** Any further activities of this nature and I will personally throw you off the team — permanently. I mean it. I don't care who it is. I will not tolerate this kind of dissension any longer."

Everyone just sat there. Finally, Liz got to her feet and said, "You just made a lot of sense. Coach, I want you to know that I am with you."

Leenie, Crissy, and Sally all chimed in, "Me too."

"Okay," said the Coach after a long, quiet pause, "let's get out on the field and get to work."

They all filed out. The blacks — Beast, Abby, and the others looked straight ahead as they silently walked to the field. Sheridan was disturbed. *How will this situation ever be resolved?*

CHAPTER 7

Mickey: The Pitcher

"That's it!" yelled Mr. Mike as Mickey whiffed in a fastball right over the plate. "I guess that's enough for tonight. You are doing really well."

Michael Mason, Mickey's dad, had been catching for her since she was barely big enough to walk and hold a glove. Mike was a catcher on the city team in the Municipal League, and every evening after dinner he would take Mickey out on the front lawn—they had no back lawn for they backed up to the Storey's place—and they would play catch. Playing catch gradually morphed into teaching her how to pitch. Fast pitch. Mickey learned the windmill and, as young kids will do, she experimented with variations of it like the double windmill—both right and left arms—and the several times around before releasing. She honed in her skills and became good at them. All those maneuvers are illegal, but she could use them sometimes in pickup games.

By the time Mickey got into high school, she was a fantastic pitcher, probably the fastest in the city. And she was accurate, too.

Her dad also bought her a drum set. She loved to play the drums and could often be heard all over the neighborhood banging away on them, booming the base drum, and clanging the cymbals. It didn't sound like fun to the neighborhood, but Mickey was having a ball. Her folks were out of town frequently, so she had lots of free, unsupervised time—not a good thing.

One Thursday as she was walking home from school, a gentleman fell in beside her, matching her strides. He introduced himself as Rolf somebody—she couldn't remember his last name. He began chatting with her—just small talk. She was a big girl and did not normally get much male attention because she intimidated most of the boys. This man seemed nice, and she was enjoying the attention. Somewhere in the conversation, he dropped the information that his "club" was looking for a drummer. He wondered if she might want to earn some money.

"What kind of club is it?" Mickey asked

"A gentlemen's club."

"What would I have to do?"

"Just show up in the evening and play the drums while the girls dance—that's all."

"I'm only seventeen," she countered.

"Whoops, I'll pretend I didn't hear that. . . . Why don't you come over tonight and check it out? I'll be there and see that nothing happens to you."

"Wait a minute," Mickey answered. "How much are you going to pay? And how many nights a week?"

" We'll give you a hundred dollars a night, cash, and you will have to show up Thursday through Sunday. Eight to one."

"What about when our ball team plays in tournaments and things like that?"

"We'll work something out."

"Well, I'll ask my Dad about it . . ."

"Mickey, I wouldn't. Old people are so fuddy-duddy, and they don't understand our younger generation and how we do things. I just wouldn't. He'll say no."

"Okay, Mr. Rolf, I'll think about it."

"Hope I see you tonight," he called as he turned and sauntered off in another direction. He hoped he had hooked her. She had been well scouted.

That evening, with her parents in Chicago, Mickey walked into the club around 8:30. It was incredibly dark inside. Several small stages were scattered around here and there. Each stage had a spotlighted brass pole. One of them had a scantily dressed girl wearing heels writhing against the pole. She was constantly moving, swaying, and dipping, and occasionally making suggestive motions. The music was canned through a sound system.

CHAPTER 8

The Gentlemen's Club: The Incident

Mickey gave her usual introductory drumroll, and a hush fell over the dark club as the loudspeaker came to life. "Ladies and gentlemen, welcome a new comer dancer tonight—her first time at the Show Club. Give a hearty welcome to the beautiful Miss Beverly St. Cyr."

As "Beverly" danced out and took her place at the pole on the tiny stage, Mickey couldn't believe her eyes. *"Beverly," my foot. That's our first baseman, Sally Thomason!* Questions raced through her head. *How did she get connected here? What exactly does she have to do?* Mickey had heard there were some "extra circular activities" the girls were supposed to take part in. Does Sally know this? Mickey didn't when she started there. Do they know how old Sally is?

Mickey kept the beat—bass drum for bumps, steel brushes for swinging, soft for dancing. Sally was doing the standard pole dance routine she had practiced at home with a CD.

The guys liked her. She was big, fresh, and somewhat shy, which rather turned them on. When a man held up five dollars, she would dance to him while he tucked it in her g-string. Another might give her ten dollars that way, and so on it went. The second half of her program was more up-tempo, and she shimmered and shook to cheers and applause. Soon it was over and she fled the floor to clear for the next dancer.

At the intermission, Mickey found Sally and confronted her. "What are you doing here?"

Sally answered with a grin, "Well, what are YOU doing here?"

"Oh, I've been the drummer here for a couple of months. I've got to tell you, though, it's like burning the candle on both ends."

"I know. It will be hard to keep our energy when we get to the finals."

"Well, I'm concerned about you, Sally," Mickey said. "Not so much on the field but in here. You take care of yourself. You are so incredibly good looking you will have all those guys lusting after you."

"Don't worry, Mick. I can take care of myself—oh, one thing, though, while we are here at the club, please call me Beverly."

Mickey grinned and nodded. "Sure."

A couple of weeks passed, and the ball club kept winning games. No one but Sheridan noticed the creeping fatigue becoming more and more obvious in both Mickey and Sally. They had lost a lot of hustle—the fire didn't seem to be there anymore. It was puzzling, but the team was winning, and they were headed for the state tournament.

One Saturday evening, Rolf caught Sally as she was on the way to her dressing room. "Beverly, there is a very important gentleman coming in tonight. He was here last night and was really taken with you. You might remember him—he gave you some pretty hefty tips."

"He slipped a fifty-dollar bill in my string, I remember."

"Well, he asked if he could meet you. As I said, he is important—and rich. If he likes you, you can benefit from his friendship. After your dance, I will introduce you to him."

"What do I have to do?" she asked.

"Just be nice to him," Rolf answered coyly.

———————

When Sally came out on stage, she glanced around the club and spotted the gentleman sitting at a table by himself, dressed in a smart, expensive suit and tie. He looked about forty-five years old. *Ugh, he is old enough to be my father.* He was looking at her, and she forced a smile. Then she swung into her routine.

"Beverly" received some paper money in her string during her dance, and it was soon over. As she came off the stage, Rolf met her, took her by the hand, and guided her to a darkened corner in the back of the club where the gentleman was waiting. In her heels, she was almost taller than he was.

"Vito," he said, "this is Beverly. And Beverly, this is Vito. Why don't you two just go in this room here and get better acquainted?" With that, he opened a nearly hidden door on the back wall and they disappeared inside.

After two other dancers performed, a loud, shrill scream come from that room.

"NOOOO. **NOOOOOOOOOOO!!!!!!!** Stop it! Then there were loud pounding noises on the door. **"Let me out,"** she cried, **"Let me outta here!!"**

Rolf was in the front lobby and heard the screams clear out there. He started toward the back immediately. What he didn't see was a man slipping out of the theater to call 911. There just happened to be a patrol car in the area, and two officers appeared almost immediately.

Everyone in the place was arrested. Mickey and Sally both got rides to the police station. In sorting it all out, the police discovered two underage girls worked in the club. With that, they came down hard with charges against Rolf and Vito—although they learned Vito was not his real name. He was Salvatore Romano, a person of interest in many crimes around the city. The police had been looking for him for a long time and had gotten lucky this time. *So had Sally!*

The newspapers inevitably got wind of the story and ran headlines like . . .

Local Girly Club Shut for Using Underage Girls!!!

The bad thing about the newspaper article was the repeated mention of the words "prostitution ring." Both Mickey and Sally were innocent of this, but the taint tends to rub off. *The good thing* was that since the girls were underage, the newspapers did not run their names.

The girls were in jail until about 4:30 a.m. when their parents came for them. Mickey's dad and mom were furious; in fact, Mr. Mason was livid. But Sally's dad just laughed, thought it was funny.

Inevitably, the word got back to Sheridan on Sunday morning. Not only the what, but also the WHO. Oh my, her star pitcher and solid first baseman. She needed them both to win at State. Should she suspend them? What should she do?

Sheridan sent word to the girls through the office that she wanted to see them both at 3:00 sharp Monday afternoon in her office.

———————

At 3:00 both girls appeared at the door of Sheridan's office. "Come in, girls, and take a seat," she said. "Let me ask you one direct question. Have you girls prostituted yourselves?"

"No, ma'am," they both replied at the same time.

"Then why in name of heaven were you there?"

Mickey spoke up first. "Mr. Rolf approached me to play the drums for their dancers and offered me a hundred dollars a night to do it. I needed the money. That is all I did, play the drums."

"How long have you been doing this?"

"About three months."

41

Slide!

"How many nights a week do you work?"

"Four—Thursday thru Sunday."

"How late do you stay?"

"I get home about one o'clock in the morning."

Sheridan realized what the fatigue factor was in her pitcher. She turned to her first baseman.

"What did you do there?" she asked

"I was a dancer, nothing more. In fact, it was when Mr. Rolf set me up with Vito that I realized how much trouble I was in. I lost my cool and started screaming. I am so glad the police arrived."

Coach sat quietly for a minute. The girls glanced at each other with quizzical looks, wondering what was coming.

Coach began slowly. "You have jeopardized the chances of this team for a successful season—maybe even the state championship. We are fortunate nothing more has gone wrong from this incident, but we must consider what could have been. I need some time to think about your punishment, but one thing is certain—you will be punished! Until that time, show up for practice as if nothing has happened. When I have arrived at my decision, you will know. Now, you are both dismissed."

CHAPTER 9

Braxton Falls: The Lecture

It was overcast the day they traveled to Braxton Falls. The wind was blowing and a small cloud of dust was swirling around the infield. Coach Matthews and Elizabeth Cornwell, the team captain, walked out to home plate for the pre-game rituals with the umpires and opposing team coach and captain.

Sheridan had just stunned everyone by announcing her starting lineup. At pitcher, Alison Whitley, a tall, loose-jointed black girl with a perpetual grin. At first base, Sharon Farnesi, a junior — a tall girl who would be first string the next year. Mickey Mason and Sally Thomason were to sit.

The first inning went smoothly enough. The Mountaineers were up first, and they went down one, two, three. Alison took the mound and seemed to be throwing well. The leadoff batter hit a grounder down to short. Melody came up with it and fired across the infield for the out. The second batter lifted a fly ball to Crissy in left, an easy play. Two down. Alison had warmed up and was feeling good, so she started bearing down. Her first pitch zoomed in for a strike. She was a little high with her next two pitches. Count 2-1. Her next pitch was right over the plate, and the batter fouled it off. Count 2-2. Alison grinned down at Liz as Liz gave her the sign. She went almost to the ground with her stretch before her windup, and then let loose a fastball that found the batter swinging at nothing but air.

In the top of the second, Beast hit a double on the second pitch. Abby struck out, but Melody singled the Beast home. Score 1-0. Melody died on base, and the score remained 1-0 until the bottom of the fifth. Then the Bears got two runs off an error by Maria at second, a walk by Alison, and a standup double by the next batter. At the end of the fifth, the Braxton Bears led 2-1.

Sheridan felt the game slipping away, but seemed powerless to do anything about it. Down at the other end of the dugout, little Caroline started talking seriously to Leenie. Caroline had taken a fancy to Melody and Leenie, who had become fast friends. The Beast pretended it didn't bother her, but it did — it irritated her tremendously that her little sister was becoming fast friends with a couple of honkies. Jealousy!

Leenie had taught Caroline some cheers, and Caroline was urging Leenie to start one. Right now. But Leenie was bashful, so Caroline just started yelling,

"Let's get fired up, fired up, fired up,

Let's get fired up, fired up, fired up

Are we fired up? Fired up? Fired up?

Yes, we're fired up, fired up, fired up."

Over and over, louder and louder Caroline shouted and even danced with the yell. With increasing energy, she spun around and pumped her arms. Her enthusiasm infected the team. Before long, they all started yelling, pumping their arms and getting the adrenalin flowing.

Sheridan was so happy to see that spark come alive, and imagine! Caroline was the leader!

Top of the sixth, Leenie came up and singled to center. She stood down on first with a wide grin. No outs. She was certain she would get around. But Alison hit a slow grounder to shortstop, who flipped it to second base, retiring Leenie. The next batter, Maria, pulled a drag bunt down the first-base line and beat it out. Two on and only one out. Sharon Farnesi, who had not played much the whole year, stepped into the batter's box. She looked relaxed as she picked up the sign from Sheridan and then sent the first pitch out of the ballpark. It sailed over the fence, clearing it by twenty feet. Sharon's heart nearly jumped out of her chest as she rounded the bases in a fog.

The game ended 3-2, Mountaineers. Another step closer to State. Sheridan called a team meeting for the next day.

————————

When they had gathered, the coach started by saying, "Everyone was aware our regular pitcher and first baseman did not play yesterday. And furthermore, everyone should be aware WHY they didn't play. They have been engaging in some highly risky activities."

Crissy held up her hand, and Sheridan nodded for her to speak. "We all know now what they were doing, but they were doing it on their own time, weren't they?"

"Yes, they were," Sheridan answered, "but whether on their own time or not, they were jeopardizing the future of this team. They were engaging in risky, unsavory behavior that might have gotten them hurt or in jail for a prolonged time, either of which would damage them and our chances at State."

"But," Crissy continued, "just driving a car across town can be risky."

"True," admitted Sheridan, "but the risk they took was unnecessary and accepted for personal gain. And the nature of the risk was in an unsavory business. This kind of behavior goes against all our principles. You girls have to understand that actions have consequences! Remember that—*actions have consequences.*" She let that last sink in a minute.

"Miss Matthews?" asked Maria

"Yes?"

"Are we going to lose them for much longer or the entire season?"

"No, they have paid their debt, and we are accepting them back on the team as of now. And I want everyone to know that our motto from here until the end of the season is . . .**Actions Have Consequences.**"

With that, Sheridan displayed a large blue banner with yellow writing on it that said just that. "This banner will be placed in the locker room for the rest of the season. I hope before you do anything impulsive, anything different, *whether good or bad*, you remember that actions have consequences."

Chapter 10

Santa Teresa: The Accident

The ride down to Santa Teresa on the bus was fun. First, they cruised along the river for miles enjoying the interesting sights and beautiful scenery. Second, from time to time, Caroline impulsively danced up and down the aisle leading cheers. This drove the bus driver to distraction and he warned her repeatedly to take her seat. But then it would happen again. She just could not sit still. She would suddenly jump up and break out into

"We got fever

We're really hot and can't be stopped

You've got the cold

And you're weak and you will be beat!"

Of course, everyone would join in the chant and then start yelling. Caroline was in her glory. Her infectious smile and pleasing manner were charming and overcame her slight speech impediment. The whole team had a warm feeling for Caroline—you might say she was more than a batgirl—she was a mascot!

One thing bothered Sheridan, however. The whites still hung around with the whites, and the blacks still mixed with the blacks. Caroline, however, seemed to be taken with Melody and Leenie. But Sheridan could see problems even with that because of Caroline's family relationship to Beast. The overt animosity seemed to be at a low point, but she felt the undercurrents of hatred and trouble were just below the surface. It worried her.

———————

The Santa Teresa Terrapins had a fast pitcher who rivaled Mickey in speed. The coaches felt the Terrapins were the last major hurdle the Mountaineers had to clear to be on the way to State in the number two seed.

In the first inning, the Mountaineers went down one, two, three. In the Terrapin half, they managed one single off Mickey, but she got the others. And so it went until the third inning when the Terrapin batters jumped on Mickey and pounded her for four hits and two runs. Score at the end of the third, Santa Teresa 2 and Shadow Mountain 0.

Maria was the leadoff batter in the top of the fourth. She ran up on the pitch and bunted it down the first-base line. The pitcher and first baseman hesitated just a second in deciding who was going to handle it, and that second, with Maria's speed, resulted in safe passage. On the way down to first, Maria dropped her bat about seven or eight feet outside the baseline.

At the conclusion of the play, the Air Force did a "fly-over" for some patriotic event downtown and everyone was distracted. Open-mouthed, they watched the loud, noisy show in the air. Caroline had never seen anything like it. It was magnificent.

Distracted at a critical time by the flyover, Caroline had forgotten the bat. The umpire called "play ball." The Terrapin pitcher went into her windup and delivered. As that was happening, Caroline suddenly realized her mistake and scurried out to pick up the bat. The timing could not have been worse. Just as she was bending over to pick it up, Beast swung hard at an off-speed pitch and sent it like a bullet, foul down the first-base line about two feet off the ground. It hit Caroline in the left temple. She dropped to the ground as if she had been shot . . . and she lay there motionless.

For a second, everyone froze in horror. Then Melody, who was in the on-deck circle, was the first to arrive at the crumpled body.

"Caroline, Caroline, are you all right?"

Caroline simply lay there. Melody looked for breathing and could find none. She felt for a pulse, tried to listen for a heartbeat. Nothing. Caroline seemed to be dead.

Melody had been trained to perform CPR, and she started on Caroline, but there was no response. Leenie was out there beside her. Sheridan rushed over and saw tears flowing from Melody.

"Is she . . .? Is she breathing?" Sheridan asked

"No, she's not."

Melody continued to work on Caroline until the ambulance arrived. The attendants quickly moved Melody aside and continued the CPR. However, they failed to get any response. Realizing the hopelessness of continuing on the ground, they picked the little girl up, placed her on the gurney, and slid her into the ambulance, where they continued to work on her.

Melody sat on the ground with tears flowing, rocking back and forth. She knew Caroline was dead.

Beast had just stood there, staring at Caroline. She had done this. She had hurt her little sister. She was devastated. It looked to her as though that little body was lifeless. She could not believe she had hurt her sister. Impulsively, she crawled into the ambulance. It whisked both girls away.

The rest of the game was a nightmare. Sheridan brought Rebecca into the game to replace Shawnaray, but the emotional damage had been done. They lost the game.

The girls sat in almost reverent silence during the ride home. Abby had called Beast on her cell phone and found out that Caroline was indeed dead. A stunned pall fell over the team.

CHAPTER 11

The Funeral: A Memorial

Caroline's mother, Eloise Norton, made the arrangements for her daughter's funeral. It was to be held at the Hogan Avenue Foursquare Church in Riverpark at 10:00 in the morning on the Wednesday following the accident.

Shawnaray did not show up at practice on Monday. Sheridan did not think much about that. She was excused for as long as it took. She needed grieving time with the family.

The funeral was a wonderful affair, a celebration of Caroline's life. Caroline had been active in the Sunday school and other church activities, and many were there to remember her. The softball team entered as a group in their game uniforms and sat in the front row reserved for them. The children's choir sang several selections, ending with Caroline's favorite, "Jesus Loves the Little Children." Caroline had been a member of that "tweenie" chorus.

Pastor Royce Martin rose and approached the pulpit.

Slide!

He noted Shawnaray was not there. He was glad he had told the recording department to make a DVD of the service for the family. The organ was softly playing in the background, "Nearer My God to Thee."

"We are gathered together here this morning to celebrate the short life of Caroline Norton and to say goodbye just as Jesus is saying hello to her. This little girl was a bright spot in everyone's life—her contagious smile, her upbeat attitude, and her helpful nature were all exemplary. Her crooked hat, her childish grammar, her sparkling sense of humor touched many lives. In her ten short years on this earth, she made many friends—scores of folks loved her. She adopted her sister's softball team and lovingly worked just so she could be near the older girls. Her personality bubbled with life and optimism."

Pastor Martin talked on about Caroline and her achievements in her short life and then prayed. "Thank you, Lord, for the life of this little one we are celebrating today. You let her life shine bright for such a short time, but we are grateful for the time you gave us with her. We know she is with you now. We ask you to comfort the family during their loss and grief. Hold them in Your hand and uplift their spirits. We ask all this in the name of Jesus. Amen."

At the end of the prayer, he announced, "The choir has asked permission of the family to do a secular song in honor of Caroline. The family agreed, and this song will conclude the service. We will gather at the graveside directly after."

As the choir rose, they started singing the verse. Everyone recognized the old popular hit, "Sweet Caroline." It started slowly and softly. Then as the song transitioned from the verse to the chorus with the words "hands touching hands, reaching out, touching me, touching

52

you" came the big crescendo buildup, walking up the musical scale. The sound built up to triple forte When they finally hit the words "*Sweet Caroline,*" the entire choir threw their arms in the air, singing at the top of their voices. They brought the volume down as the chorus ended and they started the second verse.

Again, the build-up came to "touching me, touching you." This time with the crescendo building up the scale to hit "*Sweet Caroline,*" the entire team stood and threw their arms in the air. The team members swayed back and forth with tears streaming down their faces. During this chorus, little Verlonda Johnson danced out on the platform, spinning around, dancing and swaying back and forth to the music much as Caroline had done.

When the build-up from the third verse started, the choir leader motioned everyone to stand and participate. At the point of "*Sweet Caroline*" everyone threw their arms in the air and swayed in unison. What a send-off!

Caroline's mother wept.

CHAPTER 12

The State Tournament

Mountain Shadows was seeded number one in the western region and thus drew a bye on the first game of the tournament on Tuesday night. Their opening game of the series was on Friday night, May 2, with Orchard Hills.

Sheridan sat in her office and reflected on the possibilities of the coming week. No one had seen nor heard from Shawnaray since Caroline's death. She did not attend the funeral, had not been in school, and had not attended softball practice all week. True, it had been only a week, but Sheridan was concerned. She knew grief was an individual and personal thing, but it had her playing that awful "what if" game *What if* Shawnaray withdrew from the team altogether?

Sheridan decided she should shift Darlene Travis, her freshman, to center field, and move Sharon Farnesi from the bench to right field. The major considerations were speed and batting. Leenie had explosive speed, and Sharon was a powerful hitter although she was weak defensively. Sandy Sanderson, bless her heart, still attended the practices and the games. Her crutches were gone, but she was slow in recovering her form. Sandy was just not ready yet, so Sheridan kept Melody at shortstop.

Because of the seeding, the Mountaineers did not have a particularly strong opponent in the opening round with Orchard Hills. Sheridan toyed with the idea of going with her freshman, Alison Whitley, as starting pitcher, but then decided it might be risky with Shawnaray out of the lineup. She decided she should wait for the score to develop before inserting her.

The game was to be played Friday evening in the Sports Complex at the state capital some 200 miles away. Leenie's mom, Beverly, was going to drive up alone as her husband would not return from New York until Saturday morning. Impulsively, she decided to call Gloria Gray, Melody's single mom, to invite her to ride up with her. Gloria was warmed and flattered by the invitation and readily accepted.

Friday finally arrived. Shawnaray had not shown for practice all week. It was as if she didn't exist. Sheridan had a heavy heart about the situation but felt powerless to initiate anything at this critical time. The team gathered at the high school gym at 10:00 a.m. and the players, loaded with their gear, boarded the bus to the capital. The usual laughter and banter among the girls filled the air as they wound their way east to the big city.

Beverly Travis had arranged to pick Gloria up around 2:00. She thought that during their leisurely drive down to the game, they would stop off for dinner at a restaurant she liked in Germantown. When Beverly drove up to the Gray home, Gloria opened the front door and stepped out and waved, signaling she was ready to go and for Beverly to stay in the car.

"I was wondering if this trip was ever going to happen," Beverly said with a smile as Gloria slipped into the passenger seat.

"Me too," Gloria responded. "This is so exciting. Nothing like this has ever happened in our family."

"Same with us. You know, Bob and I have wanted to have you folks over for dinner all spring, but schedules never seem to mesh."

"That would be nice," Gloria said. "Melody and I would like to have you folks too."

"Do you attend church here in Mountain Shadows?" Beverly asked.

"Well, no, we have never gotten started after the move. We used to attend the United Methodist in the town we lived in before moving here."

"We go to Grace Chapel here in Shadows and find it very rewarding," Beverly offered.

"I know. Darlene took Melody with her when we first came to town."

They rode in silence a while and then Gloria asked, "What about this girl they call Beast? Is she going to return or what?"

"I am really not sure. Darlene says she has not come to practice since the funeral."

"That's too bad, but she was, according to Melody, somewhat of a trouble maker. At least Melody had some issues with her early on," Gloria said.

"Oh, I heard about those. Yes, Beast gets into her share of trouble. Very aggressive girl. I guess that's what makes her a good ball player. I hate all those tattoos she has, though. I think they are so ugly. I don't know why young girls feel they have to do that."

Slide!

"Well, a lot of them do," Gloria replied, "so I guess you had better make your peace with it. It seems to be the 'in' thing."

"Oh, no, I am not going to, as you say, make my peace with it. It is wrong. It is terribly immature because it is so permanent. It is disfiguring, and, furthermore, it is anti-biblical," Beverly retorted.

"Really? I didn't know the Bible had anything to say against it."

"Sure does," Beverly answered. "I believe it is found in Leviticus. Let me think. Maybe Leviticus 19:28."

"I had no idea," Gloria confessed.

"Well, no disrespect intended," Shirley continued, "but that is one of the major problems of today and churches in America. I call it biblical illiteracy. People, especially many, many Christians, don't know what is in the Bible. *They never read it, they never study it, they seldom open it, yet they call themselves Christians.*"

Gloria sat in silence. The truth came crashing in on her, and her mind was grappling with the subject. Finally, she spoke. "You know, Beverly, I am one of those Christians. I almost never open my Bible and read it. I admit I don't know what is in it. But let me ask you a question. If I were to start right now reading the Bible in a continuing sense, where would I start?"

Beverly thought a minute. "I think I would begin with the gospel of John. That book answers all the basic questions in a simplified, methodical way."

"What questions are you talking about?"

"For starters, what does a person have to do to receive eternal life? We Christians call it 'saved.' Why does God want people to have eternal life? Why was the Bible written?"

58

They were about to pull up at the restaurant. The conversation ended but was not forgotten by either of them.

The game on Friday evening was an easy one. Mickey pitched for three innings while the Mountaineers were building an 8-1 lead and then gave way to the sophomore, Alison Whitley, who pitched the rest of the game.

Alison was fun to watch. She was a tall, thin, loose-jointed black girl who was constantly moving, wiggling, stretching, and hunching. And she always had a smile on her face. It was obvious she just loved to pitch. She looked as if she enjoyed every throw. In fact, Alison looked like she just enjoyed life, enjoyed being alive.

The game ended 10-2, sending the Mountaineers into the quarterfinals the next night. Their opponent, White River, won that evening also.

Sharon Farnesi hit a towering home run in the bottom of the sixth with one on to win the quarterfinals game 2-1 after trailing the entire game. White River got their run in the top of the first inning when their third and fourth batters got back-to-back doubles off Mickey. After that, Mickey settled down and took them down methodically, winning with a five-hitter.

Darlene made a sensational run-saving third out with her bases-loaded catch of a Texas leaguer in shallow left center in the fifth inning. Her blazing speed, plus her brave dive at the end to come up with the ball, cheered everyone, especially Sheridan, and justified the coach's adjusted selection.

The girls stayed the night in a local motel, ate and partied at one of the fast-food places, and celebrated before retiring to prepare for the ride home in the morning.

CHAPTER 13

Shawnaray: The Beast

They had called her Beast since grammar school. Shawnaray Norton was a big girl. She went to a school south of town that was ninety percent blacks. Her Dad took off and left the family when she was a little girl. She and her younger sister, Caroline, had been raised by her mom and grandmother. Both of them had to work, so the girls were left on their own a lot.

Shawnaray liked to hang around the playground and get involved in pick-up softball games. She was a dynamite hitter, a real power, so she was chosen high and often when the leaders were choosing sides.

She had to defend herself more than once from the advances of crude, eager young men who thought they could bully her. In a word, Shawnaray was tough. So tough, in fact, they called her Beast. They had called her Beast for so long, most folks had forgotten her real name.

All her life Shawnaray had to be on guard against people who would take advantage of her. This constant defensiveness made her wary, bitter, unhappy, suspicious, and unpleasant. She was a smart girl, but she didn't look smart, so people would mock her and try to cheat her however they could.

For the previous ten days, she had sat almost motionless in the dark. Her mind was endlessly punishing her. She had killed her little sister. *Her beloved little sister.* The one person in the world she loved more than any other. She had killed her. Her soul was in agony. She thought about suicide. No, not going to do that. Anyway, she was afraid to kill herself—actually, afraid to die. She just sat with her insides churning fiercely. After awhile, she would grieve for Caroline and cry a little inside, wondering why it had to happen.

It was Wednesday afternoon and she heard the car drive up and stop out front. Still she did not get up. Soon the doorbell rang. *Who could it be?* she wondered. Slowly, with much effort, she arose and went to the door. Peering through the peephole, she was shocked to see Melody Gray standing there. Melody? Of all people!

Shawnaray opened the door.

"Hello, Shawnaray, it's Melody."

"I know."

"Can I come in?"

"I guess so," Shawnaray said.

Melody moved into the room and sought out a chair. "Do you mind if I sit down?"

"No."

"It's so dark in here, girl. Can't we open up the curtains a bit?"

"I guess so."

Melody moved to open the curtains and let some sunlight into the room. "That's better," she said. "Everyone missed you at the memorial service last week, Shawnaray. It was beautiful. You know what? Your pastor, Royce Martin, made a DVD of the service for you."

"That's nice," Shawnaray replied flatly.

Melody thought she may as well come to the point. "Shawna, Leenie did something for me that changed my whole life."

"What was that?"

"She led me to Jesus Christ, and I accepted Him and became a Christian. She told me that Caroline was also a Christian. Did you know that?"

"No."

"We believe the Bible, and it says that when Christians die, they immediately go to heaven and are in the presence of Jesus and God. That is where Caroline is right now. We think that is wonderful."

Shawnaray broke down. She started crying and moaning. "Oh, I miss her so, I am so sorry, I am so guilty . . ."

"No, you are not guilty," Melody said forcefully. "Christians are in the hand of God from the time they commit to Him. He could have left her here on this earth, but He wanted her up there with Him. Maybe, just maybe, the reason He took her is because He wants *you, Shawna*, and He had to bring you to this point to soften your heart."

Shawna stopped crying and stared at Melody with wide eyes, "Do you really believe that?"

"One thing is for sure. When you accept Jesus into your heart, He gives you a peace, a peace that passes all understanding. Don't you feel like you need that peace?"

63

"Yes, I sure do, but I have been a bad person and God would not want me."

"Oh, yes, He does. He loves you, Shawnaray."

" I dunno. I just dunno how He could love me. How do you become a Christian?"

" Well, it is simple. So simple, in fact, that people make fun of it and ridicule it. The first thing you do is to believe in your heart—truly believe—you are a sinner because you were born that way. You must ask Jesus to forgive you for your sins. He died on the cross to pay the penalty for your sins. If you ask Him sincerely, from your heart, He will forgive you. Then . . ."

———

Out in the car, Leenie thought it was taking a long time for Mel to invite the Beast back to rejoin the team. *I wonder what is taking so long?*

Her mind was wandering further when her thoughts were interrupted by a chattering blue jay in the tree overhead. She wondered what that old jay was scolding about. Then she noticed a big, black crow fussing in the branches. *I'll bet that crow is robbing the jay's nest. Yes, that's what's happening.* Fascinated, she continued to watch the birds interact.

So many people never notice the birds. Leenie thought back to a time she was in Philadelphia in a downtown hotel. The city sounds had been blaring—horns and sirens and whistles. But then she had heard a bird in a tree outside her second floor window, singing his heart out with the most beautiful song. Such a delightful sound amid all the man-made noise.

———

Inside, the two girls finished praying together and sat quietly, enjoying the moment. Shawna turned to Mel. "What about communion? What about baptism? What about confession?"

"We'll talk about all that," Mel answered. "Shawna, there is something else I need to talk to you about too. We really need you Friday night against Overton Lake in the semifinals. It would be good for you to get out, swing a bat, and exercise a little. You know, Coach is having a fireside meeting tomorrow night at her home. Could I pick you up and bring you back home after the meeting?"

"Do you think Coach will have me back?" Shawna asked.

"Of course."

"Well, I'll think about it."

As Melody got up to leave, Shawnaray said,

"Oh, Melody, is Leenie outside in the car?"

Melody turned. "Yes, she is."

"Can I come out and tell her?"

Mel smiled, nodded, and said, "Sure you can."

———

Leenie finally saw the two girls emerge from the house and walk together to the car. As they approached, Leenie said, "Hi, Shawna."

"Leenie, I have something to tell you. I have become a Christian."

"That's wonderful, Shawna, but how do you know?"

"I accepted Jesus Christ as my personal savior, just now, inside with Melody."

Leenie thought of Romans 10:9. That was it!

CHAPTER 14

The Bonfire: The Commitment

Sheridan invited the team to her little ranchette for a BBQ, a season review, and final preparation and bonding before the semifinals with Overton Lake the next night and hopefully the finals the following night with Pine Forest. She had an ominous feeling about Pine Forest. This was a team that had not lost a game all season. They had gone 16-0. Mountain Shadows had a noteworthy record at 13-3 but were not expected to upset the Rangers.

The Overton Lake 'Gators, on the other hand, were an enigma. At 12-4, sometimes they were very, very good, and at other times, terrible. One never knew which team would show up. Sheridan realized she had better plan for the very, very good team to show up tomorrow night.

The team started arriving around six in the evening. Liz and Mickey, both seniors, were the first to show.

Sheridan greeted them warmly and ushered them to her back yard, which overlooked the whole town. It had a huge lawn, several large shade trees, and a sizable BBQ pit out in the lawn. Tables and chairs were scattered around the pit. Two older women were preparing dinner both in the kitchen and out on the grills. A pile of pinecones rested off to the side of the pit.

This gathering was simply to pull the team together, get them bonded, focused, and committed in the final run for the championship.

"Gee, it sure seems strange," Mickey said, "to realize our softball days are almost over here at school."

"I know it," Liz answered. "It just doesn't seem real."

"One of the biggest things," Sheridan inserted, "is that we are going to miss you two. You both have been such an important, integral part of this team for so long."

"We are going to miss this, too, Coach. It seems like it is such a part of our life," Liz answered.

"Here come Maria and Sharon," Mickey observed, "and Leenie and Melody are right behind."

———

As Melody walked in, she looked around expectantly but seemed disappointed when she did not see the person she was looking for. After the greetings, she turned to Sheridan. "I stopped by Shawnaray's home and invited her to come tonight. I sure hope she does, but I have a feeling she won't."

"She sure is taking this accident real hard," Liz offered.

"Oh, she is crushed, shattered. She blames herself," Melody answered.

"Nevertheless, life goes on, must go on," mused Leenie.

"She has to snap out of it sooner or later," said Sally, "but I guess a person must work through their own grief — it's a personal thing."

Soon they were all there, standing in little groups sipping lemonade or one of those electrolyte drinks, chatting and laughing about everyday matters.

"Soups on," came the cry from the cooks. Everyone lined up at the serving tables and started loading their plates.

Sheridan took particular notice of the "at will" seating arrangements. She was pleased to see they were not voluntarily "segregating" themselves as they had in the past. Abby was sitting with Sharon, Alison was sitting with Mickey and Liz, and so on. They were simply all mixed up racially. Sheridan was so encouraged.

The ribs and sweet corn were scrumptious, and the girls ate heartily. The sweet corn was especially tasty as it was the first of the season. Sheridan had ordered three ears for each girl, but they ran out anyway. Those appetites!

It was just starting to get dark when they cleared and cleaned the tables. Sheridan asked Liz, the team captain, to light the fire in the pit. The girls all pulled their chairs up in a semi-circle around the pit and gazed at the fire, almost hypnotized by the crackling flames.

Sheridan spoke. "We have come a long way, girls, yet . . . well, I guess what I want to say is we have yet to arrive. Twenty-four hours from now, you will be stepping onto the field at metro center and will be playing the games of your life. Notice I said games, not game. I am assuming you are going to win tomorrow night. That is what it is all about now. Win or go home tomorrow night. Of course, that is what it was about last weekend too, but now it is the end of the line. It is up to you.

"I have brought a pinecone for each of you tonight. Your pinecone represents you. As you throw your personal pinecone into the fire, it will burn fiery hot and light for a short time. It will be the star for the moment, and then it will settle down to be a part of the fire. I hope you can see that is how you guys are. When you step up to the plate, you are all by yourself. You will burn hot and fiery—it will be your chance to excel individually. Then when you go into the field, you will be a part of the team and work in concert with your teammates."

Sheridan turned, stooped, picked up a pinecone, and tossed it into the fire. Then she faced the girls again. "This has been the most exciting, and I must say, most challenging team I have ever worked with. I love each one of you girls. My heart is right out there with you on every play, on every pitch, on every swing. Keep your focus tomorrow night. Think, think, *think* where and how your next play will be. Then give it all you've got! Good luck."

Sheridan stooped down and picked up another pinecone and handed it to Liz, the team captain, then walked over and sat down.

Liz took the pinecone and tossed it into the fire. Then she turned and faced the team. "Well, here we are. I find it hard to believe we are playing for the state championship this weekend, but it is what we have dreamed about for four years and now it is here. In these next two days, we will be building memories for a lifetime. Let's all pull together and make those memories good ones! All I want to say now is **GO MOUNTAINEERS!**"

Liz then handed a pinecone to Mickey, who stepped to the front, accepted the pinecone, and then threw it into the fire. Mickey's voice was little shaky.

"I have been playing softball all my life. My dad used to get me out on the front lawn in the evening, pitching to him, when I was in the second grade. Never, *ever*, did I dream I would be on a team playing for the championship of the state. Wow, what an honor. I intend to do my best tomorrow night to do my part to bring it all home. I especially want to thank Coach Matthews for the second chance she gave me after I messed up. Let's go, guys, tomorrow night!" She picked up a pinecone and handed it to Sally.

Sally threw her pinecone in the fire and spoke, also thanking Coach for her second chance. Then there were Maria, Abby, and Melody. As Melody finished, she picked up a pinecone and walked over to hand it to Sandy, who was using her crutches again because of a recent fall. She hobbled to the front and gave an impassioned speech of encouragement to the team. She expressed her disappointment about not being able to play but said she appreciated being included as part of the team. When she finished, she motioned for Crissy to come up and get the pinecone from her.

And so it went, Crissy to Leenie, to Sharon, to Alison, down through the whole roster. It was dark now and the fire was ebbing to a mass of glowing coals. Sheridan noticed that not one member of the team had mentioned Beast. *They have closed ranks. They are going forward with what they have.* Sheridan was encouraged with this. *Maybe, just maybe, we will be able to call ourselves State Champs!*

The evening ended with the team yelling,

"Let's get fired up, fired up . . ."

71

CHAPTER 15

Overton Lake: The 'Gators

The semifinals! Sheridan would never get over how they had survived the quarterfinals the previous Saturday night against White River. They had won with a last minute walk-off home run by Abby. She had connected on a high fastball and sent it over the left field fence, with two runners on in the bottom of the seventh. Wow! Sheridan had thought they had little chance without Shawnaray, who still had not appeared, but the girls came through.

Beverly Travis had arranged to pick up Gloria Gray again for the trip up to the capital. The quarterfinals had been played at a 5A high school in the area, but these final two games would be played in the prestigious metro center where the professionals played, and televised throughout the state.

During their ride up, the two women chatted excitedly about their chances in the tournament and did not even approach biblical subjects. On arrival, they retired to their rooms but made a date to get together for breakfast the following morning before the big day.

When they found their seats in the stadium, the Overton Lake 'Gators cheering section was performing. The school motto was *"Are you really sure?"* This stemmed from an incident many years before after they adopted the Alligator as their mascot. The governor had said, "What are you talking about? Everyone knows there are no alligators in that lake."

To which the mayor replied with a big smile, *"Are you really sure?"*

The Overton cheerleaders pulled out a huge covered trailer with the words **Our 'Gator** in giant letters on the side. Then they "captured" a girl dressed like a Mountain Shadow cheerleader, brought her to the trailer, and pushed her in, screaming and yelling. Loud pounding and growling noises could be heard, followed by total silence. Then they sang their fight song, which ended in the yell, *Chomp'em up, chomp'em up, chomp'em up, 'GATORS!!!*

Then a grotesque figure, actually a cheerleader wearing an alligator suit, appeared from the far side of the wagon. He had a huge head, giant teeth stained with red, and green glowing eyes, with a scaly back and tail. He ran around terrorizing those out on the field. While that was going on, the cheerleader who had been "eaten" in the wagon had changed clothes, quietly slipped out the back, and disappeared. When they all returned to the wagon, the head cheerleader raised the canvas and, of course, there was nothing inside. The people in the stands howled in laughter. Indeed, she had been eaten! It was just a fun stunt.

Meanwhile, in the locker room the players were dressing. Crissy was sitting, pulling on her stockings. "Has anyone here played in this stadium before?"

"I don't think any of us have," answered Liz, "but the Overton girls play here almost every year, I think."

"They were runners up to Pine Forest last year and here they are again," said Sally.

"Can we beat them?" queried Sharon.

"You better believe it!" Mickey retorted. "This is my last chance, and I'm going after them."

Sheridan asked for quiet and started going over the signs again. She gave the same starting lineup as the previous week's game and started her pep talk.

Suddenly, the door to the locker room opened. Heads all turned to look. There in the doorway stood Shawnaray.

For a second or two, the room was silent--everyone was stunned. Then Sheridan spoke up with a warm greeting. "Welcome back, Shawnaray, come on in."

"Thank you, Coach. I was hoping I could rejoin the team."

Sheridan answered, "Of course you can, girl. We welcome you back. But, uh, I don't think we can use you tonight as we don't have a uniform for you."

"Yes, we do," spoke up Melody. "I have her uniform and shoes in my locker here. I have carried them in hope ever since she missed that game after the memorial."

Slide!

"Well, in that case," Sheridan grinned, "get suited up, girl, and join us in the loosening up exercises outside."

"Alright, girls," she started — and then stopped and grinned. "It sure feels good to have you back, Shawna." Everyone chimed in and welcomed her. Warm feelings rushed through the locker room.

Excited murmuring spread through the crowd in the stadium when number 00 stepped out on the field with the Mountaineers. Nevertheless, Sheridan stuck with her starting lineup and put Shawnaray on the bench in the dugout.

"Good evening, Ladies and Gentlemen, this is Jared Grayson, along with Jim Elliott, here to call the Final Four of the State Softball Championship Series this evening. Tonight, we have the winner of the Eastern Division, the Lake Overton 'Gators, taking on the winner of the Western Division, the Mountain Shadow Mountaineers. This is being brought to you by KCBY radio in your state capital. Starting lineup for the 'Gators is . . ."

The announcers droned on as the coaches and the team captains gathered at home plate for introductions and instructions from the umpire. The umpire was Max Shawnessey of professional baseball fame. Sheridan and Liz approached the plate and were introduced to Barbara Cannady, the 'Gators coach, and Sapphire Hanratty, the 'Gators captain.

Jared turned to Jim privately and said, "Did you hear that little girl from Shadows come over and ream me out about how I pronounced her name?"

"Sorry, I didn't hear it. What did she say?"

"She told me her name was pronounced Far-NESS-see and not what I had been saying, FAR-nah-see."

Jim laughed. "That's almost universal. 'Say what you want to about me, but pronounce my name right.'"

They both chuckled.

"Oh, I don't blame her. Her one chance in the sun here and I go and mess up her name. Go figure."

"The game is ready to start, ladies and gentlemen, as the Gators send Alicia Worthington, their center fielder, to bat."

The stadium loudspeaker cut on. **"Now batting for Overton Lake, number twelve, Alicia Worthington,"** as Alicia stepped into the batter's box to face Mickey.

Mickey promptly struck her out on five pitches. And the next batter struck out. The third batter, however, put the bat on the ball and lined one to left field, but right at Crissy, who bagged it to end the inning.

"Now batting for Mountain Shadows, number two, Maria Lopez." Maria stepped in and took the first pitch from the Gator pitcher, Dalton Briggs.

Steee-rike!!! the umpire called.

On the next pitch, Maria ran up on the ball and bunted down the first base line. Although she was fast, she could not beat out the throw from the pitcher to the first baseman.

And so it went. Both pitchers were at the top of their game. Right from the get-go, it was obvious which 'Gator team had showed up—their *very, very good one!*

Mickey struck out two in her half of the first, and the Overton pitcher, Dalton Briggs, set down the top of the

Mountaineer order easily. Thus it went on through the second inning, the third inning, and the fourth inning. The score was still 0-0. Both pitchers had allowed only two hits. Mickey had a single in the third. This time, Maria beat out a bunt right after, but Dalton was able to get Crissy to fly out to end the inning.

In the top half of the fifth, the leadoff Gator batter hit a single over second base, a solid hit. The next batter laid down a perfect bunt. As Mickey came off the mound to pick it up, she turned her ankle and fell. Liz was right there and picked up the ball, but both runners were safe. Mickey was down quite a while, but she worked through the pain and slowly got to her feet. Sheridan considered taking her out, but Mickey pleaded to stay in, so that's how it was.

Mickey's first pitch after the injury was hit right out of the ballpark. Score 3-0, Overton. Sheridan thought, *This doesn't look good at all. Perhaps I should take her out. I dunno, I'm not sure, but it is up to me to decide . . .*

Jared spoke rapidly into the microphone. **"Folks, it appears that Mickey Mason is really hurt. When she put weight on that ankle in the pitch, something came off the pitch, and the batter sailed it over the fence. Wait, here comes Coach Matthews out to the mound. Her catcher, Liz Cornwell, and third baseman Abby Anderson are also out there with her. They are having a rather heated discussion. Well, there it is, Coach Matthews has motioned for her backup relief itcher to come in. That would be Alison Whitley, a sophomore right-hander. Oh, wow, imagine getting the call to come into a championship game as a sophomore reliever!"**

Mickey had argued but to no avail. She knew she was injured, but she wanted to stay in. However, that last pitch told her, told everyone, she belonged on the trainer's table, not on the mound in a championship game.

Sheridan made the necessary reports to the umpire and the loudspeaker system blared,

"Now pitching for Mountain Shadows, number seventeen, Alison Whitley."

After a few warm-up throws, Alison nodded that she was ready, and the umpire yelled, "Play ball."

"This little girl looks like she is having fun, Jim. Look at that smile on her face. Here is her first pitch — piped down the middle and taken by the batter. Strike one."

Alison worked her way through the batters and managed to get out of the inning without further damage. The score was still 3-0, 'Gators. The score held in the top of the seventh inning.

In the bottom of the seventh inning, the Mountaineers were batting from near the bottom of their lineup. Leenie hit the ball hard but right at the third baseman, who threw her out. Alison then struck out. So with two out, Maria Lopez, top of the order, stepped up to the plate. The shortstop was playing in for a bunt and got fooled. Maria stroked a little blooper over the shortstop's head for a single. Crissy Watkins was at 1-2 and the pitch got away from Dalton and hit Crissy in the shoulder. She went to first, sending Maria to second.

Sally Thomason came to the plate. Sally took two strikes with the bat on her shoulder. She was waiting and hoping for "her pitch." The next one was it. She hit safely into right field, but the right fielder was up with the ball in a hurry and held Maria to third with a really good throw. Bases loaded.

Slide!

"Sharon Farnesi is due up next with bases loaded, folks." Jared announced. *"What drama! Wait a minute, here comes Sheridan Matthews out to the umpire. It looks like there is going to be a batting change."*

"Now batting for Mountain Shadows, number zero zero, Shawnaray Norton.

"My goodness. This girl has not played for two weeks. She was involved in a tragic incident in a ball game two weeks ago in which her little sister was killed. And here she is stepping in—at a most dramatic time. Bottom of the seventh, two outs, three runs behind, and bases loaded. You could not write a movie script like this that anyone would believe. This is incredible."

Emotions welled up in Shawnaray. *I would like to get this one for Caroline. What an opportunity, what a chance! Perhaps God has worked this out for me. Who knows?*

Dalton shut out the base runners from her mind. The bases were full. She concentrated on Shawnaray. She had a three-run lead. She could focus on getting the batter. Dalton went into her windup and delivered, putting everything she had into the pitch. Shawnaray swung at it like, *like a beast!* She missed. Strike one.

Dalton felt a little more confident now. She wound up and delivered the second pitch—outside, ball one. Dalton walked back behind the mound, rubbing her hands with the resin. Stepping on the mound, she delivered the next pitch and Shawna hit a high pop fly curving foul and out of play. Count was 1 and 2. The next two pitches were low and outside.

"The count is 3 and 2 on Norton now. Full count."

Shawna's face was grim and resolute. She swung the bat back and forth a couple of times waiting for the pitch. Now she stopped and took her stance. *And the pitcher threw . . .*

"Norton hit the three and two pitch, OH MY! It's a towering high fly ball to straight away center. Oh, IT'S GONE! IT'S GONE! IT'S GONE!" Jared yelled. "It cleared the fence out in deep center by thirty feet. She hit a grand slam homer!!! The Mountaineers win the semi-finals!! Incredible, incredible."

It had felt fantastic to Shawnaray, and she savored the feeling as she trotted around the bases. The gang was waiting for her when she came into touch home plate with tears streaming down her face. Hugs, high-fives, cheers. The Beast had hit a walk-off grand slam. Final, 4-3, Mountaineers.

When Shawna got into bed that night, she whispered, "Thank you, Jesus."

CHAPTER 16

The Breakfast: A Frank Discussion

Gloria Gray, Melody's mom, and Beverly Travis, Leenie's mom, met outside the motel rooms and decided to walk over to the restaurant. As they were arriving, they met Royce Martin and his wife, Angela, with Eloise Norton, Shawnaray's mother, and Emogene Williams, her grandmother. After greetings, they all entered the restaurant and sat together at a single round table.

"We were so excited to see your daughter back last night," Beverly said, "and thrilled at her hit to win the game."

"Thank you," replied Eloise. "I am so grateful to Pastor Martin here and also to your daughter, Melody."

"Why my daughter?" a puzzled Gloria questioned.

"Well, your daughter led my daughter to Jesus."

"I didn't know that."

"It happened last Wednesday afternoon. I was down

83

to Jessup-town. When I came home, I found Shawnaray sitting reading the Bible. The curtains were open and the house was light—that was a first time since Caroline's accident. She seemed calm and at peace with the world. We talked awhile and she told me what had happened that afternoon, with Melody coming over and all."

"Well, then, I guess I should ask," Royce Martin said, "why me?"

"Oh, Pastor, you know it was you who talked Shawnaray into coming up here last night and pumped the courage into her to approach the team."

"Well, that young lady did it all on her own," he countered. "I am so proud of her."

They ordered and sat chatting while drinking coffee. Gloria wanted to ask Royce Martin a question and finally got up the courage to do so.

"Reverend Martin, I was wondering what version of the Bible you would recommend?"

"Well, several translations are good. Usually people not too familiar with the Bible start with the King James Version. That version is a reliable, good translation, but it is four hundred years old and uses words in many places that are no longer used or understood. Some other translations offer more clarity."

Beverly inserted, "What is your favorite, Reverend Martin?"

"Please, ladies, drop the reverend thing. Just call me Pastor Royce."

"Okay, Pastor Royce, what is your favorite translation?" Beverly repeated, smiling.

"My favorite is the American Standard Version of 1901, but there are others. There is a New King James that purportedly "fixes" all the archaic words. And there also is the New American Standard Version that does about the same."

"What about the NIV?" Beverly asked

"That one, the New International Version, has become very popular and is a wonderful modern translation. I was reading the testimony a while back of a man in Australia who has led many, many people to Jesus with the NIV."

"I have noticed," Gloria said, "when we stop at motels, the Bible in the room is a King James. Why is that?"

"Most Bibles placed in motel rooms are done so by the Gideon Society, and they pretty well stick with the old King James. It is a very old society and tradition dies hard. You know, aside from the archaic words and phrasing of the old King James, another problem lurks in its use."

"What's that, Pastor?" Eloise asked.

"It is so full of 'thee and thou, thine, wouldest and shouldest, and uncommon words like verily and perish and — oh, I could go on and on and list dozens of them. Some people get to thinking it is some kind of a *holy language they must use when they pray or talk to God or about God or else they are not spiritual.*"

Gloria got a strange look on her face, laughed a nervous laugh, and confessed, "I thought it was. I am learning something here. I did think there was something holy and spiritual about the thee's and thou's."

"Well, it is not true," Royce continued. "God is your heavenly Father, and you can speak to him in your everyday language. Respectfully, of course, but everyday language. Shakespeare lived during the time the King James version was translated. We don't talk in Shakespearian English, do we? It would sound absurd, dumb, stuffy, and pretentious."

Their breakfasts came and they settled into eating their fare. The discussion moved away from Bible translations to everyday things like current prices and living expenses, and even the weather. Soon the breakfast was over and they went their separate ways until the game that night.

Beverly and Gloria set out to go shopping.

Chapter 17

The Finals: Pine Forest

Mickey Mason slumped morosely in her uniform on the trainer's table as the trainer taped her ankle. They had been fussing with it for a half hour. First, the shots, and then the movement analysis, and now the taping. Fussing, fussing, fussing. She had had heat treatments all day, followed by this ice for an hour before the game. She wondered if they knew what they were doing. One thing was for sure, it didn't hurt. She wanted to get out there and try it.

It was about thirty minutes until game time. She should be warming up. Finally, the trainer stepped back and said, "I guess you are ready, girl. I want to wish you good luck. If it starts to really hurt or bother you, come back in and we will see what we can do."

The stadium was filling up. Exuberant Mountain Shadows fans gathered on the third-base line behind the Mountaineer's dugout. This was the first time the Mountaineers had ever been to the softball finals.

"Good evening, ladies and gentlemen. Welcome to

Walker Memorial Stadium. Would you all please rise for the national anthem?"

The teams had assembled on their respective baselines and were standing erect. When the song started to play, everyone on the field promptly removed their hats, put their hands over their hearts, and stood quietly. The anthem was being sung by a talented young man. On the last note, everyone started whooping it up. Sort of a tradition nowadays.

"Good evening, ladies and gentlemen. Jared Grayson here, along with Jim Elliott, to call the finals, the championship softball game of the season between the Pine Forest Rangers and the Mountain Shadow Mountaineers. The starting lineups for both teams are as follows . . ."

———

Sheridan had put Shawnaray back in center field and moved Leenie to right. She convinced herself that Mickey was ready to go so went ahead and put her in the lineup.

The pre-game ceremonies at the plate were the usual introductions and review of the rules by the umpire. The home team was decided each year by a formula, and this was the year for the Western Champions—the Mountaineers—to be home team. Soon everyone heard the familiar call from the umpire to **"PLAY BALL."**

The leadoff Ranger batter stepped in against Mickey, and Mick delivered. Ball one, outside. Mick's windup and pitch, the ball was hit to the second baseman. Maria scooped it up and threw her out. Mickey seemed to be okay on that ankle, and her pitching was certainly up to par, so Sheridan started to relax about that. But the team seemed to be flat, no spark. And there was no question this was a very, very good Ranger team.

In the Mountaineer half of the inning, the batters went down one—two---three.

In the second inning, Mickey handled the Rangers again—the heavy hitters—without incident. But then the same thing occurred in the bottom of the second. And the third, and the fourth, and the fifth, and the sixth, and the seventh. These teams were tied at the end of regulation seven innings at 0-0.

"Ladies and gentlemen, we are checking the record books for we believe this has never happened before, a nothing to nothing tie at the end of seven in a championship game," Jared said. "This is one ding-dong pitchers' battle out there tonight."

Megan Sarnosky, pitching for the Rangers, and Mickey Mason for the Mountaineers both looked sharp. The problems were at the plate. The batters all seemed so flat and frustrated they could not get solid wood (or aluminum) on the ball.

The pitchers were not striking everyone out. On the contrary, the batters for both teams were hitting the ball, but not square. Foul balls, pop ups, shallow flies, innocent grounders, and bloopers were occurring. The frustration level of both coaches was rising. Something had to happen.

In the top of the tenth, it finally did!

The first Ranger batter drew a walk. Mickey protested vehemently, but of course, to no avail. The second batter laid down a bunt. Mickey let Abby charge it and make the quick throw. Too late. Two on, no outs. The next Ranger batter hit a sharp ground ball down to Abby, who picked up and fired to Maria, who then turned and fired to Sally. Double play. Two down now. But the runner on second moved up to third. Danger here. Watch for an attempted steal.

"Now batting for Pine Forest, number seven, Cele Brown."

As fate would have it, the batting champion of the league was up next, a home-run hitting right-hander. Sheridan moved her fielders over—Crissy almost down the line in left, Shawnaray positioned in left center, and Leenie far over to center in right, leaving right field virtually unprotected.

"Ladies and gentlemen, this could be the end of the ball game if Cele Brown gets any kind of a hit here," Jason theorized. "And Cele is the state batting champion, so look out!"

———

Mickey was getting weary. She had thrown a lot of pitches. She stood motionless, looking at the batter step into the box. Liz went into her crouch and flashed the sign. Mick started her windup and delivered. It was a ball. Second pitch—Mickey tried to jam her with a fastball, hoping for the inside of the plate.

"Steeee-rike!" the umpire yelled.

Liz flashed the sign for a change-up. Mickey wound up and gave her a change low on the outside of the plate. Cele saw it coming, tried to hold up, then realized she had better swing, and hit it hard—the ball went high in the air down the right field line. It looked like it was going to be fair.

Sheridan's heart sank. Then she pulled her eyes down from the sky and saw Leenie on the run. Leenie was all-out, giving it all she had, sprinting to the ball. As the ball descended, it looked like Leenie was not going to make it, but at the last second she dove, totally stretched out horizontally — giving her body up. She stuck that glove out there and plop! *She made the catch* and did a somersault, coming up with the ball in her glove.

The Mountain Shadows crowd went crazy. Cheering, yelling, clapping, laughing, screaming. Hey, Pine Forest — it's not over yet!!!

In the bottom of the tenth, Leenie was the leadoff batter.

"Now batting for Mountain Shadows, number eleven, Darlene Travis.

"Ladies and gentlemen, this is the girl who just made that sensational catch out in right field. Here she is coming to the plate."

The Ranger coach called time and walked out to talk to her pitcher, Megan Sarnosky.

"Be careful here, Meg. This girl is high as a kite right now after making that play. Look at that grin on her face. Don't give her a whole lot to hit. Don't put her on if you can help it, but keep the ball away from the center of the zone," the coach pleaded.

Sarnosky nodded and walked away, putting resin on her hands.

Leenie took the first pitch, low and outside — ball one. She looked at the second one and it looked too high. Ball two. The third pitch came inside just above the knees for a strike. The next one was a change-up but way outside. Count was 3-1.

Sarnosky tried to bear down on the next pitch, but it floated up around the shoulders and Leenie walked.

Slide!

Mickey was trying to bunt but hit a pop fly to the shortstop—one out. Maria also tried to bunt but popped it up right back to Sarnosky. Two out.

Sheridan was frustrated. She realized her own pitcher was getting tired; in fact, everyone was getting tired. Sheridan decided to try to end it right then. She flashed the sign to Leenie and Sally, who was coming to the plate for a hit-and-run play. Leenie acknowledged. Sally acknowledged.

Sarnosky delivered. Leenie took off as soon as the ball left the pitcher's hand, and Sally swung hard on the pitch and connected with a sharp single to right field, curving toward the corner. By the time the right fielder came up with the ball, Leenie was rounding second base and charging for third.

Sheridan decided right then—*let's go for it!* As Leenie was coming all out getting ready to slide, Sheridan dramatically waved her home.

"Travis has rounded second and is charging toward third. Her coach is WAVING HER HOME!! Oh my, this is going to be close." Jared was shouting.

Leenie's eyes got big as saucers when she realized she was being waved home. The throw was already in the air going toward third as Leenie turned and sped toward home with all she had. Sheridan cupped her hands and shouted to her, "Go, girl, go!!!"

"Travis has rounded third and is charging the plate. The Ranger shortstop is cutting off the throw and turning to throw to the plate. The Ranger catcher has moved up the line a few steps to block the runner coming down," Jared reported in rapid-fire talk.

Leenie was coming as hard as she could. How was she going to get in there? The catcher had moved up the line to block her. Should she just run right into her and try to knock her over and make her drop the ball? *I don't think so,* she thought. *That catcher must weigh 180 pounds.*

Leenie saw Shawnaray, who was on deck, standing back behind the plate but lined up so she could see her as she came down, motioning frantically with her left hand for her to move over and with her right hand to slide.

Execute a slide-by? I have never done one, she thought — her mind working a thousand miles a minute. *But then I guess there is no other way. I'm gonna go for it!*

Jared was screaming into the mike now . . . *"HERE COMES THE RUNNER, HERE COMES THE THROW. IT'S GOING TO BE CLOSE!"*

At the last instant, Leenie moved over about a foot and a half but still in the baseline and launched her body into the air to begin the slide. She hit the dirt with a cloudburst of dust. Umpire Max Shaunassey was standing right over the play, leaning in to see it close-up. The catcher caught the ball and in the same motion swung to tag Leenie, but Leenie had moved over just enough to make the catcher miss her. The umpire saw the catcher's glove had missed Leenie by about an inch. The umpire quickly snapped his head to the right to watch Leenie as she slid by the plate. Leenie reached out and slapped home plate as she caromed by. Done deal. The umpire's arms shot out to the side — palms down — in the classic movement as he shouted, "S A F E !!!"

"IT'S OVER! IT'S OVER! SHADOWS HAVE SCORED. THE MOUNTAIN SHADOW TEAM HAS WON. THEY ARE THE NEW CHAMPIONS!"

Slide!

After the award ceremonies, the on-field celebrations carried on with tears, hugging, congratulations, and both team and individual pictures with trophies. Then the girls just stood around in the afterglow. Friends and relatives gathered around them, chatting excitedly.

Sheridan and her assistant went up to the office to gather their papers and equipment. They sat down for a minute to enjoy the joy of victory.

"What is it going to be like next year?" asked Margo.

"I am not sure, hon. We are losing six seniors, but the bright spots are Alison, Darlene, Maria, Crissy, and Pat Smalley — all of them will be back — plus the girls coming up from the junior varsity."

"What about Sandy?"

"Of course, Sandy will be back for sure. I think that leg will have totally healed, and she is a real sparkplug."

"Think we can do it again?"

"We are the returning champs. We are going to go for it!"

It was interesting that most of the Overton Lake team had stayed overnight for the game and were actually rooting for Shadows. A few of the girls had become friendly with Mickey and Sally, so no one thought anything about their spending time chatting, nor had any clue they were cooking something up.

After the team retired to the locker room to shower and meet family, a couple of Overton girls swung into action. One of them dressed in the alligator suit while the other helped get it on properly. They covered the alligator then with a sheet so as not to be discovered and went

94

down to the Mountaineers' dressing room. They had to stifle their giggling and get serious to do this stunt. Outside the door, they could hear the winners inside still celebrating as they showered and dressed, hollering and laughing.

On the count of three, they burst open the door and the alligator went charging into the locker room, making all sorts of loud, grotesque growling noises and grabbing at the players. The girls were first stunned and shocked, and then started screaming and shrieking. It sounded like a massacre in there.

———————

Up in the coaches' office, Sheridan and Margo were finishing gathering their things when they heard all the screaming and yelling. Sheridan grinned. *Girls will be girls!*

THE END

&

If you have enjoyed reading *Slide*, please take just a few moments to leave a review online at your favorite book retailer. Your comments are greatly appreciated by the author and future readers!

Fireflies

God's Lessons on the Farm

Fireflies is not a book about flying insects but rather about tiny flickers of God's illumination opening our spiritual eyes to His lessons in nature. This is a fresh approach to a Christian devotional book. Happenings on the ranch and farm are related as they actually occurred. The spiritual applications, as the author felt impressed upon him by the Holy Spirit, are unusual. His insight gained from associating with animals and plants in their living processes is both entertaining and enlightening. The author's fascinating stories are not necessarily in chronological order, but they do encompass the broad, practical side of country life and show how it relates to all of us in our Christian experience. As a man's spirituality is one of the most personal and private aspects of his life, the author has courageously chosen to share some of his special experiences with you.

The Top Ten Crucial Mistakes of Young Pastors

(and some older ones, too!)

In his hard-hitting, no-punches-pulled, aggressive style, Ron Stout "calls them as he sees them." His goal? To help young pastors focus on the most important aspects of their ministry. His method? Delivering a comprehensive, progressive list of pastoral mistakes he has observed over his lifetime.

The rankings of the mistakes are Ron's alone. You may not agree with him on the positioning of the mistakes, but you will probably agree they all belong somewhere on the list. Ron's editor comments that the book is "...not only directed to pastors young and aged but also to the church as the body of Christ." Use *Top Ten Mistakes* as a classroom text, a study guide, or a handy reference. Or read it just for enjoyment.

Westward Ho!

Randall, a blacksmith, and his wife, Shari prepare to head West in 1859. Elliot, Randall's younger brother, is at a crossroads in his life as the Civil War is looming in the East. Elliot does not want to be a soldier, so he signs on with the newly formed Pony Express and is relocated to Wyoming. The entire family joins a Mormon wagon train to start an exciting new life with perilous adventures along the way. Westward Ho!!!

Spike!

When twins Vangie and Evie Anderson discovered beach volleyball, a whole new world opened up to them. With the support of their parents and coaches, their long hours of practice pay off. Simultaneously, the girls and their mom become popular as a gospel trio, singing mostly in churches as featured vocalists. But they were not without their critics, and their lives were not free of setbacks and challenges. How would the girls find the right balance between gospel singing and their volleyball careers? Join Vangie and Evie as they grow up and learn how to determine God's plans for them and His priorities for their lives.

Ringer

Alicia Bradley loved horses and dreamed of being a great jockey. She seemed to be well on her way to riding stardom when she innocently became embroiled in an underworld plot which threatened her personal freedom for life. Her choices of behavior were questionable and resulted in additional angst. However, she followed her heart in a serious romance. Reas how her life changed radically, but in the latter years she felt she would not have changed one minute of it.

ಬಂ

To purchase any of these titles, send a note stating the title(s) you want, along with a check payable to Desert Rim Ministries; add $4 for shipping. You may contact the author directly at PO Box 1100, Willcox, AZ, 85644, or ronstout85644@gmail.com. His books are also available at most online retailers.

Made in the USA
Middletown, DE
27 August 2023